The PERSIAN CINDERELLA

Shirley Climo • art by Robert Florczak

HarperCollinsPublishers

Long ago, when Persia was a land of princes and poets, there lived a maiden named Settareh. Her name meant "Star," and it was given her on the day she was born because of a star-shaped mark on her left cheek.

Settareh had scarcely opened her eyes to see or her mouth to cry when her mother died. Although she lived with her stepmother, two stepsisters, three aunts, and four female cousins in the women's part of the house, she was often lonely.

Settareh seldom saw her father, for he was busy in the world of men. Her stepmother and aunts ignored her, paying no more heed to her than to a fly on the wall. She belonged to no one, and nothing belonged to her. She wore her stepsisters' cast-off clothes and ate their leftovers, sometimes finding only melon rinds to fill her dish. Even so, Settareh grew lovelier with the years.

The brows above her dark eyes arched as gracefully as the path of an arrow, and her long black hair gleamed like polished ebony. She was delicate, with slender ankles and tiny feet. But her beauty only added to her misery, for it made her stepsisters jealous.

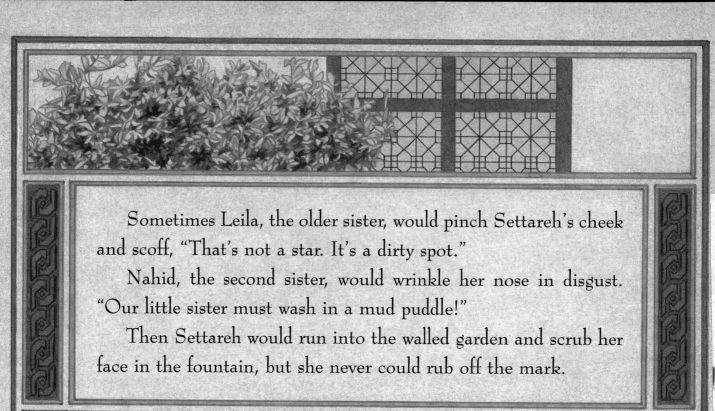

Sometimes Leila, the older sister, would pinch Settareh's cheek and scoff, "That's not a star. It's a dirty spot."

Nahid, the second sister, would wrinkle her nose in disgust. "Our little sister must wash in a mud puddle!"

Then Settareh would run into the walled garden and scrub her face in the fountain, but she never could rub off the mark.

One morning in late winter, Settareh's father honored the women's quarters with a visit.

"Prince Mehrdad invites all to the Royal Palace for *No Ruz*, the New Year," he announced. Opening his money pouch, he gave everyone a large gold coin. "Buy cloth in the bazaar to make new clothes," he told them. As he handed Settareh her coin, he patted her hand and added, "Choose wisely."

Each girl and every woman, no matter her age, covered her head with a cloak so that no stranger might look on her face. Then, like a flock of blackbirds, the mothers, daughters, sisters, and cousins flew down the road to the marketplace.

The bazaar's covered street was lined with shops and crowded with animals and people. Goats bleated and donkeys brayed. Merchants hawked pearls drawn from the waters of the Persian Sea, and traders shouted prices for silks brought by camel caravans from faraway China. Carpets woven in jewel-like colors brightened the walls, and the scent of ginger and cinnamon from the Indies and perfumed oils from Egypt hung in the air.

Settareh sniffed something familiar, too. "Toasted almonds!"

She turned and saw a peddler stirring a pan of nuts over a brazier. She'd had nothing to eat that day, and her mouth watered. Shyly, Settareh held out her gold coin. Quickly, the peddler snatched it. He gave her a wrapper of warm almonds and a handful of small silver coins in return.

Settareh finished the nuts in two mouthfuls and then counted her money. "I can still buy cloth," she said.

She pushed through the crowds, anxious to find her family again. But as she hurried, a wrinkled woman tugged on her cloak and held out a brass bowl.

"Spare a coin, young mistress," she begged.

Settareh hesitated. The old lady was shivering, and her robe hung in tatters. "You are more in need of new clothes than I, grandmother," Settareh said. Opening her fingers, she let most of her coins clatter into the woman's bowl.

"Good fortune come to you," the crone cried. "And soon!"

Settareh smiled and looked down at her remaining coins. "At least I may buy a new sash," she told herself.

As she hastened past a pottery stall, Settareh saw a small jug lying in the dust. It was made of ordinary clay and a jagged crack ran down one side, but it was glazed with a blue as bright as the sky. Settareh could not take her eyes from it.

"That pot—is it for sale?" she asked the shopkeeper.

He peered at her. "It is worth much . . ." he began.

Settareh couldn't resist picking up the jug. It felt as warm to her touch as something alive. "This is all I have." She offered him her last three coins. "Please."

The shopkeeper sold Settareh the little blue jug.

Her stepsisters could not believe what Settareh had bought with her money.

"A leaky old *pot!*" squealed Nahid.

"Now you'll have nothing new to wear for *No Ruz*," Leila scolded. "That's unlucky! You will disgrace us!"

"Then I shall not go to Prince Mehrdad's festival," Settareh retorted. But she feared she had not chosen wisely. *No Ruz* was only eight days away.

The New Year began on the first day of spring. Already the snow that iced the Alburz Mountains was melting beneath the midday sun, and many-colored wildflowers carpeted the hillsides. Inside the women's quarters, everyone was busy measuring and cutting and stitching their new clothes. Settareh sat alone in the garden, listening to the call of a turtledove in the pomegranate tree and holding her little blue jug.

"I don't care if you are cracked." Settareh rubbed the pot with her finger. "But I wish you were filled with jasmine blossoms."

The jug began to quiver and her fingertips tingled. Suddenly the air was sweet with fragrance, and her jar brimmed with white flowers.

"Magic!" she gasped. On the outside, the jug looked as always. On the inside, perhaps . . . a *pari*!

If the fairy granted one wish, would it grant another? "Please, little jug," Settareh whispered, "I am hungry."

A basket of figs and apricots appeared before her.

Then she said, "Little jug! I am cold," and at once she was wrapped in a warm shawl of the softest goat hair.

She said, "Little jug! I am lonely." The dove flew down from the tree, perched on her shoulder, and cooed in her ear.

Settareh did not ask for more, fearing her stepmother and stepsisters might notice. The *pari* in the jar was her own secret.

The eve of the New Year, Settareh watched while the others paraded in their fine new clothes.

Leila smirked and smoothed her sea-green dress saying, "It is too bad you cannot attend Prince Mehrdad's festival, Settareh."

"She would rather stay here and talk to her old pot," Nahid said, for she had spied her stepsister whispering to it.

Settareh did not answer, but as the gate of the courtyard swung shut behind the others, she picked up her blue jug. "Would you kindly give me a gown for *No Ruz*?" she asked.

The jug in her hands grew warm and began to jiggle. When it stopped trembling, a dark red silk dress, the color of ripe pomegranate seeds, was spread before her. Beside it lay a golden pendant to hang about her neck, and turquoise bracelets to wear on her wrists. Best of all, there were two small diamond-studded anklets to sparkle at her ankles.

Settareh patted the jug. "Thank you," she said. Then she dressed quickly and covered her head with a scarf, and said, "I am ready to go."

One magic moment later she found herself outside Prince Mehrdad's palace. Settareh climbed the marble staircase and glanced timidly into the arcade on her right.

A handsome youth stared boldly back at her, smiled, and stroked his beard. Settareh clutched her scarf to her face and fled through the arcade on her left.

She found herself in a huge hall filled with women. They sat on silk cushions and helped themselves to heaping trays of roast lamb and whitefish, to spiced cucumbers, sweet oranges and tart rhubarb, and to goblets of sherbet cooled with mountain snow.

Musicians plucked tunes on lutes and zithers, and cymbals rang as dancers twirled. Magicians juggled flashing knives, and snake charmers from India coaxed

cobras from their baskets. Poets rhymed verses, and fortune-tellers read the future from their star charts.

No one recognized Settareh. She kept her head bent and her star mark hidden. Even Leila and Nahid, dazzled by her finery, believed her to be a princess from some distant land.

When the rushlights burned low, the music and amusements ended. "How could time fly so?" cried Settareh, dismayed.

She would pay a dear price if her stepmother returned and found her bed empty. Settareh fled from the palace, running through the twisting streets. In her haste, she did not feel a diamond bangle slip from her ankle. She did not hear it splash into the shallow canal that flowed beside the road. She did not discover her loss until she reached home.

All night the anklet lay in the ditch. But in the morning, the sun shone on the water and made the diamonds flash. A horse, drinking from the ditch, snorted and reared.

"Steady!" shouted the stableboy, tugging the reins. He fished the anklet from the water. "I must show this to my master."

"Extraordinary!" the Horse Master exclaimed, blinking at the band of diamonds. "I must take this to the palace."

"A tiny treasure!" Prince Mehrdad declared, dangling the bangle from his finger. "I must find the one who wore it."

"How can a man look for a maiden?" asked Mehrdad's mother, the queen. "What do you know of women and their ways?" She rose. "I myself will find the owner of that anklet."

The queen ordered her bearers to carry her curtained palanquin to every household in the city. In each, she bid the women to put on the bangle. "Prince Mehrdad wishes to meet the maiden who can wear it," she explained.

Young and old tried to squeeze into the anklet. They pushed their heels and pulled their toes until their feet were pinched and purple, but not even the thinnest among them could put it on.

At last the queen called at the house where Settareh lived. One after another, the stepmother, aunts, and cousins failed to force on the anklet. Although Leila and Nahid cleverly oiled their feet, they still could not wiggle their slippery toes through the band.

"Enough!" the queen snapped. As she turned to go, Settareh appeared wearing the red dress, the gold necklace, and the turquoise bracelets.

Settareh crossed her arms over her chest, bowed to the queen, and said, "Please allow me, Exalted One."

Without difficulty, she eased her foot through the diamond bangle. As her stepmother and stepsisters stared in disbelief, she lifted the hem of her gown and revealed the matching anklet.

"Come," said the queen. "The prince awaits you at the palace."

"One moment . . . if you will," stammered Settareh. She hurried to fetch her little jug from the garden.

Leila followed and pinched her arm. "How?" she demanded.

"There is a *pari* in my jug. I need only wish." Pulling away, Settareh ran to the queen's palanquin.

The queen gave Settareh a mirror so that she might gaze at the prince's reflection without the embarrassment of facing him. Settareh peered into it and caught her breath. She had seen those eyes . . . that smile . . . even the beard before. Now he wore a tulip-shaped turban, but this was surely the man she had glimpsed at *No Ruz*.

Mehrdad stared back. "Settareh!" he exclaimed. "Star!"

Settareh had forgotten that he could see her image in the looking glass too. Quickly she covered her cheek with her hand.

"No!" Prince Mehrdad pulled her fingers away. "Your mark is heaven-sent. The stars foretell that we shall marry."

Settareh knelt and touched her head to the ground. Then she looked up at him and said, "You honor me."

The queen summoned Settareh's father to arrange the marriage. For thirty-nine days the entire kingdom celebrated. Settareh invited her stepsisters to join the festivities in the palace, but even that did not please them. They grew more jealous and vengeful with every passing day.

On the fortieth morning, Leila grumbled, "Today is the *agha*, the wedding ceremony. Settareh will become a princess!"

"Why not me?" Nahid threw a cushion at the palace cat. "Why not you?"

"Perhaps," Leila murmured, "if Settareh were gone . . ."

"Then the *pari* would help *us*!" Nahid squealed.

The sisters looked at each other and giggled. "Why not?"

While Settareh strolled with the queen in the palace garden, her stepsisters slipped into her room, pried open her chest, and snatched the little blue jug.

Leila held it up. "Listen," she ordered, "we want Settareh gone—forever! Give us a way to be rid of her!"

The little blue jug shuddered. It grew so hot that smoke seeped through its crack. "Help!" Leila screamed, dropping it. The jug shattered, and scattered among the bits of blue clay gleamed six jeweled hairpins.

"Ah!" said Nahid, picking them up. "Special pins . . . for our special sister."

That afternoon, the stepsisters smilingly offered to arrange Settareh's hair for the ceremony. First they washed it in scented rose water and then they brushed it until it shone.

"Married women must pin up their hair," advised Leila. She coiled Settareh's hair at the nape of her neck and pushed in one of the pins.

"Ouch!" cried Settareh.

"How clumsy of me," Leila said. "Let me try again." She thrust another pin into Settareh's hair, and another, and another.

"Please . . ." Settareh began, but her voice grew weak.

"Five . . . six . . ." Nahid jabbed in the last hairpins. "Done!"

With those words, Settareh vanished. In her place trembled a small gray turtledove. It cooed mournfully and flew out the palace window.

"Where is my Star?" Prince Mehrdad demanded. "I cannot find her."

"Settareh has flown," Leila giggled. "But we are here."

Nahid smiled and said sweetly, "Why not choose one of us?"

"None can ever take her place!" cried the prince.

He ordered searches throughout all of Persia, offering rewards for her return. But Settareh was nowhere to be found.

"Aie! Aie!" Prince Mehrdad moaned, plucking hairs from his beard in anguish.

He shut himself within his royal chamber and saw no one, not even the queen. He refused the delicious dishes brought to him and grew thin and pale. His only companion was a turtledove that often came to his window. The bird was shy, but the prince was patient, and after many months it let him stroke its head. Beneath the bird's feathers, the prince felt hard bumps.

"Hairpins!" the prince exclaimed. "How strange!" He gently pulled one out. "I shall try not to hurt you, small friend."

The turtledove sat quietly while he drew out four more hairpins. As he removed the sixth one, the bird fluttered and gave a cry. Prince Mehrdad cradled it in his arms—and then discovered it was not a dove he held.

"Settareh!"

Withdrawing the last pin had broken the spell.

At the wedding ceremony, Prince Mehrdad and Princess Settareh sat on a gilded couch as one thousand matched pearls were showered upon them.

Leila and Nahid watched with bulging eyes. Their cheeks burned with jealousy. They puffed up, sputtering with spite, until they were so filled with rage that their hearts simply burst.

That was the end of them and of their spite. But it was just the beginning of happiness for Settareh, the Persian Cinderella.